A LENNY AND

TROUBLE ON THE TRAIN

CW01657658

HAZEL TOWNSON

Illustrated by Philippe Dupasquier

Andersen Press · London

First published in 1997 by
Andersen Press Limited,
20 Vauxhall Bridge Road, London SW1V 2SA

All rights reserved. No part of this publication may be reproduced, stored in a retrieval system, or transmitted in any form or by any means, electronic, mechanical, photocopying, recording or otherwise, without the written permission of the publisher.

Text © 1997 by Hazel Townson
Illustrations © 1997 by Philippe Dupasquier

The rights of Hazel Townson and Philippe Dupasquier to be identified as the author and illustrator of this work have been asserted by them in accordance with the Copyright, Designs and Patents Act, 1988

British Library Cataloguing in Publication Data available
ISBN 0 86264 624 3

Phototypeset by Intype London Ltd.
Printed and bound in Great Britain by
the Guernsey Press Co. Ltd., Guernsey, Channel Islands

Contents

For Libby Tempest

Your library is precious – Use it or lose it!

1
Momentous Journey

The great day had arrived! Miss Pritchard, accompanied by the mothers of Erica Carr and Patsy Huggins, was taking her class on the train to Manchester to visit the science and transport museums . . . or at least, that was her intention. Little did she know what crisis was in store on that never-to-be-forgotten journey!

On the way from school to Cobston

station, Lenny Hargreaves and his friend Jake Allen walked at the end of the crocodile, aiming to keep as far from Miss Pritchard as possible, though they could not avoid Mrs Huggins who was bringing up the rear.

'I bet this is going to be pretty boring,' grumbled Lenny, who had never entered a museum in his life. The very word was enough to put him off.

'It's bound to be better than school,' replied Jake more hopefully. He was looking forward to the train journey at least, as he had never been on a long-distance train before. He had also heard a rumour that in the transport museum you could actually take a ride in a scaled-down model of a space-craft. Unreal!

In the station booking-hall Miss Pritchard counted her charges carefully, then preached a final sermon about good behaviour, which needed to be no less than perfect in the presence of members of the public.

'Don't forget, children, that you are representing Cobb Street Primary School today. We don't want to let our school down, do we?'

'No, Miss Pritchard!' came the reluctant chorus.

Lenny Hargreaves groaned. He had already eaten most of his packed lunch, and the prospect of a day's good behaviour was doing nothing to cheer him up. His only consolation was that he had some magic tricks in his pocket, which might come in handy to brighten things up if the going got really tough. Lenny's ambition was to have his own magic show on television one of these days, and to that end he was constantly practising tricks on his long-suffering friends. He was hoping today would be no exception.

At last the train came in. Miss Pritchard had reserved a whole compartment for her party and despite her sermon the children piled hurriedly and noisily on board with a great deal of pushing and shoving. Lenny

MANCHE
RESERVED

and Jake, who did more than their fair share of this, managed to find seats right at the far end of the compartment, so that they would have a good opportunity to vanish through the sliding door every now and again.

In fact, the train had hardly started before restless Lenny suggested a tour of exploration.

'No; wait a bit. I want to look out of the window.' Jake was enjoying the sight of Cobston streaming away into the distance and once he had grown tired of that, he planned to read his comic. Being the eldest of six children, Jake did not have many treats, and even the comic was a one-off luxury specially provided for the journey.

Lenny sat sulking for a while, then he leapt to his feet, declaring: 'Well, I'm going to snoop around a bit!' He was beginning to think Jake Allen was turning soft, and felt that the sooner he spurred the lad into action the better. He scrambled over Jake, who was sitting next to the passageway, and slid open the door.

'Lenny Hargreaves! Where do you think you're going?' boomed the voice of eagle-eyed Miss Pritchard from the other end of the compartment.

'To the toilet, Miss!'

'Oh, very well. But hurry up, and come straight back here.'

Lenny escaped with a sigh of relief and proceeded to lurch his way through the next compartment and along towards the buffet car. His mother had given him five pounds extra for the trip on top of his usual pocket money, and he thought he might study the buffet price-list.

There was a queue already forming at the buffet, so Lenny joined it. He found himself standing right behind two men who were talking together earnestly. They looked like businessmen, each wearing a smart suit, one brown, one grey.

Lenny had always wondered what businessmen talked about, so he listened in shamelessly . . . and was amazed to find himself hearing news of a sinister plot.

'Where've you planted your time-bomb, then?' asked Grey Suit.

'It's between Welshaw and Stockport,' came Brown Suit's muttered reply. 'Hundreds of casualties, I'm afraid, but it can't be helped.'

'Oh dear! I can just see the newspaper headlines!' Grey Suit spoke with mock regret. 'Once they find out who's behind it, you'll be the biggest villain since Jack the Ripper!'

'Can't be helped, I'm afraid. That's the way things are these days. Innocent people have to suffer. I guess we just have to harden our hearts.'

Lenny could scarcely believe his ears. This very train, travelling north at this very moment, was scheduled to stop at Welshaw and Stockport on its way to Manchester. So his entire class, plus all the other passengers, were sitting there like sacrificial victims, just waiting to be blown to bits! Wide-eyed and open-mouthed, he turned and ran back to his own compartment.

2

A Bomb on the Line?

Lenny Hargreaves hurtled down the aisle to the seat occupied by Miss Pritchard. In his frantic urgency he even grabbed that lady's arm and shook it whilst blurting out his message.

'Miss, there's a bomb on the line, somewhere between Welshaw and Stockport, which is right where we're going! It's a time-bomb. I just heard these men talking about

WEAVERHAM HIGH SCHOOL LIBRARY

it and they said there'd be hundreds of casualties. They said it couldn't be helped and they had to harden their hearts. We've got to do something quick, Miss, or we'll all be killed.'

Miss Pritchard firmly removed Lenny's hand from her arm. Then she took a deep, deep breath before declaring: 'Lenny Hargreaves, I have been planning this outing for weeks and I don't intend to have it disrupted by any of your mischievous pranks. We all know your love of the limelight, not to mention your vivid imagination. How can you possibly think you've discovered something that the whole of the vigilant railway staff has missed? You had no business to be listening in to other people's conversations in the first place, let alone misinterpreting them and repeating them to other people. I thought you were just going to the toilet? Now, sit down and behave yourself. I'm going to ask Mrs Huggins to keep a special eye on you.'

'But, Miss, it's true! You've got to believe

me! I heard every word . . .'

'I said SIT DOWN, Lenny! If you don't like the seat you've chosen you can always come and sit next to me.'

Lenny realised with a sinking heart that it was no use trying to explain any further to Miss Pritchard. For the sake of dodging trouble he had told her so many tall stories during his school career that now she was suspicious of everything he said. Still, he didn't intend to sit on the train and get blown to bits either. He and Jake would have to sort things out themselves.

With a last despairing glance at his teacher, Lenny hurried back to his seat and began whispering the whole story to his friend.

Jake was only half-listening and didn't even look up from his comic. 'Ah, go on with you!' was all he said.

'It's true! I've just told you everything word for word as I heard it.'

'Baloney! Real terrorists wouldn't stand about discussing bombs in a place where anybody could overhear. Except in comics, of course. There's sure to be another explanation. Those men could have been talking about something else, and you've just got the wrong end of the stick.'

'Something else such as what?'

Jake sighed impatiently. 'How should I

know? I'm not a businessman. Anyway, there's one way to find out for sure. Those two aren't going to blow *themselves* up, so if they're still on the train when it leaves Welshaw, then you'll know you were wrong.'

'If we wait that long it might be too late. Suppose they intend to jump clear at the last minute?'

'That's a bit far-fetched. Anyway, if Pritty won't believe you nobody else will either. So I don't see what else you can do but wait.'

'Huh! Some help you are!'

'What, just because I don't see sinister folks round every corner! You're potty; you know that?' grinned Jake, turning over the page.

This started Lenny off on a fit of the sulks. He scowled, fretted and fidgeted for a good half-hour, until eventually the train pulled in to Welshaw station. This brought Lenny back to life. He immediately pressed his face to the window to observe the alighting passengers, and suddenly he leapt excitedly out of his seat.

'What did I tell you? There they are!' he shouted, snatching Jake's comic away and forcing him to look out of the window. 'See? That's them! They *are* getting off, and they're both in a mighty hurry!'

It was true! Brown Suit and Grey Suit were actually running down the platform at great speed, weaving their way nimbly among the other passengers. Brown Suit had a briefcase clutched to his chest, while Grey Suit carried a parcel.

'Just look at 'em! They can't get away from this train fast enough!'

'Maybe they're late for work.' All the same, Jake reluctantly began to wonder if there was something in Lenny's story after all. Grown-ups didn't usually dash about like that. Besides, a parcel was a pretty suspicious object these days; it could contain anything, including a detonator or a lump of Semtex explosive.

Jake rescued his comic and folded it carefully away. 'What we gonna do, then?'

'Well, I'm not wasting any more breath

on Pritty, so I guess we'll have to warn the conductor instead. Come on!'

At that moment several Welshaw passengers with heavy luggage entered the compartment, not realising it was already full of children. In the confusion Lenny and Jake managed to escape into the next compartment without being spotted. There, they began frantically trying to find help before the train moved off.

3

The Passengers Protest

Luckily, the boys came across the conductor almost at once, as he was helping an old lady to her seat.

'Hey, Mister!' Lenny wasted no time in blurting out his story excitedly, but the conductor was not impressed. He looked Lenny up and down with a critical eye.

'Trying to make mischief, are you?' he demanded without even a ghost of a grin.

'Hoping to liven up a boring journey, I suppose. You're from that school party in Coach C, aren't you? Well, I think I'd better go and have a word with your teacher.'

'You'd be wasting your time, Mister,' Lenny assured him hastily. 'We've already told her the tale, but she doesn't believe us.'

'Sensible woman!'

Just then Patsy Huggins appeared, calling after the boys from the end of the compartment.

'Jake and Lenny, you just come back to our lot right away before the train sets off. My mum's supposed to be keeping an eye on you, and if Pritty finds out you've gone again you'll get my mum into trouble.'

'I'm not going anywhere till I've sorted this out,' Lenny called back stubbornly. 'And you can tell your mum that me and Jake are trying to save her life, not to mention the lives of everybody else on this train, even yours.'

These words had an ominous ring, and as Patsy disappeared in a huff the old lady suddenly spoke up.

'I think you should give the boy the benefit of the doubt,' she told the conductor. 'He looks a decent lad to me, and you never know what might happen these days. We hear such awful tales.'

'Yes, but madam . . .'

'If you don't check, and then something goes wrong, you'll have it on your conscience for the rest of your life. If you've still got a life, that is.'

'Now, let's be reasonable, madam! I can't go passing on a ridiculous tale like that with absolutely no proof. I'd start a terrible panic, and all for nothing. You know what young lads are like, especially when they get over-excited. Best thing to do is to ignore the whole thing and get on with enjoying your journey.'

'I should just think so!' cried an angry-looking man with a black beard. 'Kids like that are just out to make trouble.'

The conductor turned to go, but was confronted by a woman from the seat behind the old lady.

'I don't know how you can talk about enjoying our journey after a rumour like that!' she protested, leaping to the aisle. 'It seems to me that everyday life is turning into one great terrorist nightmare. Nobody knows what's going to happen, from one minute to the next.' She turned to address those around her. 'I don't know about the rest of you, but this latest tale sends shivers up my spine. Did you see that episode of "Casualty" the other week, the one about the train crash . . .?'

'Rubbish!' cried the bearded man, whose name was Gritz. 'And if you let these kids disrupt our journey . . .!'

'It wouldn't do any harm to check,' a man across the aisle interrupted him quietly. 'Perhaps the conductor could ring in for advice. He can borrow my mobile phone if he likes.'

'Yes, and then what? Then we'd get held up for hours on end while they made a check,' Gritz spluttered furiously. 'Some of us have better things to do than sit here all day.'

Suddenly another elderly passenger stood up. 'I'll have you know,' he announced to the whole compartment, 'that I was in Warrington that time they tried to blow up the gas works. And only a few days after that there was a bomb in the centre of the town. That's certainly made *me* ready to give the benefit of the doubt in future.'

'Well, I hope you all realise that this gentleman's right,' sighed the conductor, gesturing at Gritz. 'If I do make a fuss it will mean holding the train here at Welshaw and searching the line all the way to Stockport. Goodness knows how long that would take.' There were some murmurs of protest and annoyance at that, but the old lady declared loudly: 'Better safe than sorry, as I think the majority agrees. And hadn't you better hurry up, young man? We'll be starting off in a minute.'

'We can't start off until I give the signal, madam!' The conductor was trying hard to keep his patience. In the end he turned to Lenny and Jake.

'I think you two had better come along with me to see if we can sort this out.'

Before the boys could protest he had ushered them out of the compartment and away towards the rear of the train.

'Just a minute, Mister! We'd better tell our teacher where we're going!' Lenny protested. 'Our coach is the other way.'

'Yeah, we'll be in big trouble if we don't,' added Jake. 'And he's in enough trouble already.' ('As usual,' he added quietly to himself.)

'You should keep your noses out of other people's business then, shouldn't you?' suggested the conductor. 'But now that you've made this accusation and stirred up all the passengers I'll have to do something about it. We'll need to go along to the guard's van and have a telephone discussion with the powers that be. Maybe they'll want to speak to you. And you needn't worry about your teacher; I'll certainly be having words with her in a minute.'

Although this sounded slightly ominous, Lenny began to enjoy himself. He was sure he would be proved right in the end, and felt quite important, being ushered all the way through the train by the person in charge. Everybody was looking at them, and besides, he and Jake were about to get a privileged view of the inside of the guard's van, which would be something to boast about to the rest of the class. They might even persuade the conductor to let them have a go on the intercom.

It was a very long train. They must have plodded their way through seven or eight coaches before they finally came to the guard's van, and the first thing they saw in there was a tandem cycle. This was an unexpected bonus; definitely a five-star experience. Lenny had never seen a tandem close up before and was already wondering if the conductor might let him and Jake sit on it, just to get the feel. He stared at the machine with interest, storing up every detail to relay to his friends and family. (All good practice, of course, since magicians have to train themselves to be observant.)

The tandem looked like a brand new machine. Even the tyres were spotless and the saddles were so highly polished you could see your face in them. Lenny began lovingly to stroke a bulging real leather saddle-bag from which dangled a destination label proclaiming GRITZ – MANCHESTER.

The conductor picked up a telephone and began speaking in a weary voice.

'Briggs here. You're not going to believe this, but we seem to have a bit of trouble brewing . . .'

Jake, who was listening in, guessed it must be the train driver that Mr Briggs was speaking to, in which case trouble was definitely brewing. Lenny was probably wrong as usual, and maybe the pair of them would get thrown off the train. Even if that didn't happen, Pritty might be so cross that she would dump them in the Left Luggage office at Manchester and collect them again on the way home. As Jake began to surface from this nightmare, Mr Briggs was saying:

' . . . And you don't even want to question the kids? Righto then, we'll be on our way.'

Mr Briggs replaced the receiver, made an apologetic announcement over the intercom,

moved to the door and gave the signal to start the train.

Unfortunately, this was the moment when Lenny yielded to temptation, grasped the front handlebars of the tandem, gave the brakes an affectionate squeeze and disturbed the balance of the machine. The starting train did the rest. There was a crash and a cry of dismay as the machine collapsed on top of Lenny, but that was as nothing to

the cries of Mr Briggs when he realised that the front handlebars of the fallen machine had been bent and the front wheel well and truly buckled. As if that were not enough, one of the tyres had split, and a fine white powder was spilling gently out of it.

Spluttering with rage, Mr Briggs seized Lenny by the collar and hauled him to his feet.

'Just what d'you think you're doing?

Haven't you caused enough trouble for one day?'

Yet before he had time to let his anger really take off, the door of the guard's van flew open and in rushed the bearded passenger called Gritz. Maybe he possessed the gift of second sight, for that tandem belonged to him. Was he in such close communion with his machine that he could sense its danger? He was certainly furious to see the damage that had been done, and his complexion took on an alarming shade of purple as he leapt to examine the machine and let go a stream of curses. Yet bad as it was, this situation hardly justified Gritz's next move, which was to produce a gun from an inside pocket and point it menacingly at the boys.

'Don't any of you move, or I'll shoot!' he cried, placing himself protectively in front of the fallen tandem.

4

A Plastics Factory Drama

A few minutes earlier, just before the train left Welshaw station, Brown Suit, who was, in fact, Mr Donald Dacre of Dacre Plastics Limited, had leapt breathlessly back on to the train to recover his umbrella which he had left behind on the luggage rack. His seat had been the one now occupied by the old lady, who immediately recognised him from Lenny's description.

'Here, just a minute, young man!' The old lady laid a restraining hand on Mr Dacre's arm. 'I believe the conductor wants a word with you.'

Mr Dacre began to protest that he was late for a business meeting and must hurry, but by this time several other passengers had realised what was going on, and had gathered round, effectively blocking his exit.

'The conductor just needs to check something with you.'

'It won't take a minute.'

'Might save us all a lot of time.'

Someone was sent off to fetch the conductor, but at last, as there seemed to be no sign of him returning, either with or without Mr Briggs, the man with the mobile telephone repeated to Mr Dacre the words which Lenny had overheard. As he did so, quite a menacing little group of passengers gathered round, insisting that the suspect should not leave until the matter had been thoroughly investigated.

Mr Dacre began to laugh, though somewhat nervously.

'You can't possibly believe I'm a terrorist! Me, of all people! Surely you can see it's just a silly misunderstanding? I admit I did say those words, but they didn't mean what you think. I happen to be in the Plastics business, and I was talking about a couple of branches of our firm, one in Welshaw and one in Stockport. We shall have to close one branch down, owing to the poor business situation at the moment, and that will mean making hundreds of people redundant. Those were the "casualties" I was talking about. If you don't believe me, you can ring my office on this number.' He handed a business card to the man with the telephone.

There was a moment's silence while the significance of this sank in. Several passengers leaned over to catch a glimpse of the card, which was eventually passed around. Then everyone began talking at once, some in sheer relief, others indignant at the upset caused, and all of them anxious now lest the search of the line had already been organised.

'We don't want our journeys delayed. I've got to catch a connection.'

'Better find the conductor quickly and tell him what's happened.'

However, before this could be done, an announcement was made over the intercom by that very conductor, to the effect that the train would be leaving at once with apologies for the delay which had been due to a slight misunderstanding.

'Great! He's already checked and found out it's a false alarm.'

'Kids!' sneered someone in disgust. 'We might have known!'

'Mind if I go, then?' Mr Donald Dacre did not wait for an answer but scrambled off the train with his umbrella. He was only just in time as the train began to move out of Welshaw station.

At that very moment Patsy Huggins's mother

was reporting to Miss Pritchard that Lenny Hargreaves and Jake Allen appeared to be missing once more.

'I'm going to walk along the train to look for them,' she decided.

'Not before time!' snapped Miss Pritchard. 'Those two need watching EVERY MINUTE, Mrs Huggins, believe me! When you find them, I want a word with the pair of them, and they'll come and sit here with me for the rest of the journey.'

'I know which way they went,' whispered Patsy to her friend before disappearing in the opposite direction to that which her mother had taken.

5
Ambush

Halfway between Welshaw and Stockport lay a wide expanse of open countryside; fields full of rabbits, strips of woodland, the occasional farmhouse and hillsides dotted with sheep. It was in one of the strips of woodland, which ran right along both sides of the railway line, that two men called Josh and Joey were crouching close to the track. Each was dressed in black jeans and jersey, and had a black balaclava pulled tightly over his head and face. The only parts of them that showed bright as berries among the trees were two pairs of anxious eyes. With guns at the ready, they were waiting to hold up the Manchester train.

'Right, Mr Clever-Gritz!' Josh whispered gleefully. 'Four minutes to go, and you're in for a big surprise!'

'Can't wait to see his face!' grinned Joey.

'He'll have a heart attack, I shouldn't wonder!'

'Reckoned he'd thought up the perfect hiding place for his drugs, didn't he? Well, he's gonna fold up and DIE when we leap into that van.'

'Last thing he'll expect is us lying in wait for him.'

'He was a fool ever to think of taking the stuff by train. Once he'd decided to pack it into that tandem, he'd have done better to get some help and ride the blessed thing.'

'Nah! Couldn't do that. He's even crammed packs of the stuff in the tyres, so he couldn't very well risk a puncture.'

'Hollow frames, hollow seats and tyres as well? That's some amount, that is! I reckon we've really hit the jackpot this time!'

Josh glanced at his watch. 'We have if Lecky behaves himself with that signal. Mind you, he's a pretty cool customer is Lecky. Right now I wouldn't be in his shoes for all the burgers in McDonald's.'

Despite this hint of risk, the mission had been carefully planned. Days of painstaking work were to culminate in a neat bit of split-

second timing. The minute Lecky heard the train approaching, he was to put a black bag over the green signal and hoist a red lamp in its place. If running to time, the train would then stop in this remote and sheltered spot at exactly nine minutes past ten, Josh and Joey would leap into the guard's van, grab the tandem and bundle it into their own van, now hidden among the trees. From there, a neat series of vehicle switches would take them to their hideout in Manchester where they would dismantle the machine, rescue the drugs so cunningly concealed in the machine's hollow parts, and make a fortune from the distribution of those drugs in local pubs, schools and discos.

'Let's not count our chickens yet,' warned Josh. He knew that everything – especially the vehicle switches – depended on split-second timing. Any delay to the train could ruin the whole operation. And what if Gritz changed his plans and decided to get off the train at an earlier stop? Joey reckoned he'd only do that if he became suspicious, and surely there wasn't much chance of that. They'd all been very careful. Of course, they hadn't reckoned with the likes of Lenny Hargreaves and Jake Allen, and if Josh and Joey had known what was happening in the guard's van of the Manchester train at that very moment *they* would have been the ones to collapse with shock.

Back in the guard's van, Lenny Hargreaves was staring into the muzzle of Gritz's gun. He felt hypnotised, unable to move or think. He was jerked back to life by the sound of Gritz's voice:

'Right! You two sit down back-to-back and keep quiet!' Gritz ordered, indicating the dusty floor. He walked over to a huge pile of dirty white canvas, beside which lay a coil of rope. He picked up the rope and wound it round and round the boys to bind them together. He was just working on the knots when there came a loud, urgent hammering on the connecting door.

'Quick! Have you got a first aid kit?' somebody shouted. 'This old bloke's fallen in the toilet and cut his head. There's blood all over the place.'

For a second, Gritz hesitated. He hadn't quite finished dealing with the boys, but he knew it would look suspicious if the conductor didn't respond immediately to this call.

He motioned for Mr Briggs to answer the door.

'See what they want. But no funny business, or you won't live to tell the tale. I'll be right behind you. You don't say a word to anyone, and you come straight back here afterwards. Understand?'

Turning to the boys, he hissed: 'Don't you dare try to move or make a sound. Nobody would hear you, even if you did. We'll be back in no time, and Briggs'll be very sorry indeed if you've caused any trouble, because he's the one who'll get shot first.' In actual fact Gritz wasn't a bit worried. What could two scared young lads do against a hardened

operator like himself? What could *anyone* do against the power of the gun?

As further shouts and knockings began, Mr Briggs grabbed his first aid kit from a shelf.

'Give me your keys!' demanded Gritz. Carefully he himself opened the door just a fraction, so that no one could see in too far. With a last threatening remark to the boys, he then ushered Briggs out, following him closely, and locked the door behind them as they went off with the man who had raised the alarm.

A few seconds of stunned silence passed before Lenny whispered: 'Phew! That was a stroke of luck! He's not had time to tie the knots properly. I bet they won't stand the strain. Start wriggling, quick!'

Jake groaned. 'Lenny, you heard what he said. That bloke's a real nasty, and if we cause any trouble . . .'

'Once we're out of this rope we'll cause some trouble all right. We'll have surprise on our side.'

'Just think what you're doing, Hargreaves! That man's more dangerous than World War Three. You're not playing Year 6 football now.'

'I *know* what I'm doing. I'm tackling one problem at a time. You didn't think we were just going to sit here and wait to get shot, did you? The stuff in that tyre must be drugs. That's my guess, anyway. And we've seen it so he's not going to let us go. Start wriggling, I said.'

Jake knew when he was beaten. He sighed and started wriggling.

It was true that the rope was not too securely fastened. After a few moments' vigorous movement the boys managed to loosen it a fraction. Then with much straining and groaning Lenny pulled one arm free, then the other, and soon both boys were standing unfettered among the discarded coils of rope, wondering what to do next.

'We could yell for help,' Jake suggested.

'He said nobody would hear us, and I bet

WEAVERHAM HIGH SCHOOL LIBRARY

he's right. This far away you'd have a job to hear anything above the noise of the train.'

'What about the intercom?'

'Oh, sure! First thing he'd do when he heard that would be to lose his temper with that gun. We'll need to think of something a bit more subtle.'

'Well, let's be quick about it!' Jake was alarmed at the thought of the gun, and was now wishing desperately that he had ignored Lenny's antics in the first place, and had stayed in his seat, peacefully reading his comic.

Suddenly Lenny had a brainwave.

'I know! When Gritz comes back I'll distract him with one of my magic tricks.'

'Oh, no!' Jake glanced pleadingly up to heaven. If all they had to depend on was one of Lenny's magic tricks, then they might as well make their wills.

Lenny plunged an eager hand into his pocket and came out with his latest acquisition, the Flying Flounder trick. Once he had arranged this carefully, he suggested that they should climb back into the coils of rope, sitting back-to-back again with scared and miserable faces, as if their bonds had never been disturbed.

'Then when His Nibs comes back we'll see what that nifty little Flying Flounder can do.'

6
Blood and Panic

Meantime, some distance away along the train, Mr Briggs was mopping up the blood from a cut on the head of the old man who had fallen. It was quite a nasty cut, and one of the onlookers suggested it would need stitches.

'Shouldn't we stop the train and get an ambulance to take him off to hospital?'

'No, no; there's no need for that!' Gritz interrupted hastily from his position right at

Briggs's elbow. 'Head cuts always bleed a lot and this one isn't very deep. He'll be perfectly all right when he gets bandaged up. Then we'll help him back to his seat and give him a cup of tea. He's just told us his daughter's meeting him at Stockport, so she'll be able to take him to her doctor if need be.'

'All the same, the usual procedure in a

case like this . . .' began Mr Briggs, who was anxious to stop the train at any price.

'We're running late already,' insisted Gritz with a deal of menace. 'Best thing by far is to get the old gentleman delivered up to the bosom of his family. We'll be in Stockport in no time.'

'Well, I still think . . .' began Mr Briggs bravely.

Through the cloth of Gritz's jacket pocket the gun eased its way into the small of Mr Briggs's back.

It was a tense and significant moment and Briggs caught his breath. What happened next could affect all these people's lives. Perhaps it was just as well that an interruption came.

'Excuse me!' At the very moment of crisis Mrs Huggins pushed her way through the knot of bystanders, grabbed the conductor's arm and spoke urgently to him. 'You've got to help me. I'm looking for two young boys. They seem to have vanished; I can't find them anywhere on the train and I'm getting really worried.'

Mrs Huggins began to describe Lenny and Jake, whereupon Gritz looked straight into her eyes and told her he remembered seeing those two boys get off the train at Welshaw.

Mrs Huggins reeled with shock. 'Oh, goodness me! I don't know what their teacher's going to say!'

'Well, you'd better go and tell her, hadn't you?' Gritz suggested coldly as he increased the pressure of the gun on Briggs's back.

7

Patsy to the Rescue

Patsy Huggins lurched her way up to the guard's van just as Gritz was shepherding Mr Briggs back into it.

'Here, where do you think you're going?' he demanded, barring Patsy's way. 'Passengers aren't allowed up here.'

'Our teacher's sent me to fetch two boys back. I think they came to the guard's van with the conductor. She says they've to come back with me right away.'

'Well, they're not here!'

'They must be. I've walked right along the train and they aren't anywhere else.'

'I've already told your teacher, they got off the train at Welshaw.'

'No, they didn't. They wouldn't dare. Oh, go on, Mister!' Patsy wheedled. 'If I don't get those two back to their seats they'll be in really big trouble. You wouldn't want that, would you?'

Meantime inside the guard's van Lenny lay in wait with his Flying Flounder trick. This consisted of a huge silk net displaying the skeleton of a fish in luminous paint. This net, being made of the finest silk thread, could be tightly packed into a flesh-coloured container not much bigger than a thimble, which Lenny, at the right dramatic moment, would flick into the air from apparently nowhere. A frying-pan (in which to catch the flounder) also formed part of this trick, though unfortunately Lenny did not have that with him or it might have made a pretty handy weapon.

'What use do you think that's going to be?' Jake had already asked, eyeing the Flying Flounder with disgust.

'I should have thought that was obvious.'

Lenny's hands were out of action under the rope, but the minute the door opened he spat the net viciously from behind his teeth. It soared through the air, spread itself out like some giant, man-eating cobweb and came to rest on Gritz's face.

'What the . . .?' Gritz struggled to wrench the Flying Flounder net off his face, making such athletic contortions that two things happened. First he was obliged to release his hold on Patsy, then something heavy fell to the floor.

'Get him, Puggins! He's going to shoot us!' yelled Lenny, leaping desperately from the sabotaged coil of rope.

'Grab his arms!' roared Jake, leaping after Lenny.

Gritz was really angry now. He tore away the Flying Flounder, wrecking it for ever, then intended to swing round, hoping to rescue his gun from the floor.

The only thing that stopped him was a voice behind him that cried blithely: 'Stick 'em up!' as Patsy Huggins prodded him in the back with something cold and hard.

8

The Spinning Spider

Gritz assumed that Patsy had picked up his fallen gun and was now holding it to his back, so he slowly raised his hands, playing for time until he could think of his next move. A kid like that was hardly going to have the nerve to shoot him, but it was a delicate situation that needed care. After all, accidents could happen.

If only Gritz had known, Patsy was in fact prodding him with a pen. She had seen the gun, but had more sense than to touch it in case the nasty thing went off. The gun had slid behind her, so she knew Gritz was unlikely to see it unless he turned round. Patsy's job was to stop him doing that.

'One move, and I'll shoot! My dad taught me how, and he's the best shot in Cobston,' she threatened, trying her best to sound wickedly confident.

'That's the stuff, Puggins!' Lenny encouraged her triumphantly. Even as he spoke, he was untangling the rope ready to tie up Gritz with it.

By this time the startled and bemused Mr Briggs had pulled himself together. He was the one who leapt to gather up Gritz's gun and was now dragging Patsy to safety.

'We've got to stop the train!' he yelled, preoccupied now in covering Gritz with that man's own weapon.

'Leave it to me!' cried Jake, leaping eagerly to pull the communication cord, which was something he had wanted to do all his life. So had the rest of Cobb Street

Primary School, and probably every child in the civilised world. He would be the envy of them all!

With a satisfying tug Jake brought the emergency handle down. There was an almighty screech of brakes and the train ground to a halt.

Lenny was furious. If anybody had to pull the communication cord it should have been him, and he doubted if he would ever forgive Jake for this. After all, he, Lenny, was the one who had saved the day with his Flying Flounder trick. But for that, Jake Allen might have been dead. He couldn't have pulled any communication cords then!

But this was no moment for argument. Gritz had realised he was beaten, and was making a desperate attempt to escape. He didn't think Briggs would be much more of a shot than Patsy, so now that the train was stopping he intended to risk jumping out. He made a great leap towards the door, but he had reckoned without the world of magic.

Lenny Hargreaves would never have thought of setting out for a whole day's adventure with only one magic trick. He had a couple more in his pocket, favourite of which was the Spinning Spider, a huge, black plastic Tarantula which now spun through the air with a high-pitched screech and landed on the back of Gritz's outstretched hand. Gritz was horrified. He had a terrible fear of spiders and fell backwards with a scream as he tried to shake the nasty black thing from his hand. As Gritz fell, he banged his head on the fallen tandem and knocked himself out.

'How about that?' yelled Lenny. 'Any idiot can stop a train, but only a skilled professional magician can stop a villain.'

By this time, some other railway official had rushed to the door demanding to know why the train had stopped, and in no time Gritz had become a struggling prisoner.

While all this was going on, Lenny seized his biggest chance of all. He had missed out on pulling the communication cord, but he was jolly well going to fulfil another ambition. His voice was soon heard over the intercom announcing that there was no need to panic, the train would be starting off again very soon, and apologies were offered for any inconvenience caused.

'That's Lenny Hargreaves's voice!' Miss Pritchard cried. 'Just what does he think he's up to? When I lay hands on that boy, he'll wish he'd never even heard of a trip to Manchester.'

9

A Sneak Thief Foiled

In Belfield Woods Josh and Joey were growing restless.

'That train's ten minutes late now!'

'There must be something wrong!'

'Yeah, you don't suppose he's been rumbled?'

'Oh, not Gritz! He's too experienced for that. And he's armed, don't forget.'

'Accidents can happen. Somebody might have got suspicious and passed the word on.'

'Well, we'll just have to wait and see. We'll give it another five minutes.'

'But you said it was no good if the train was late.'

'Look, we've been over these plans a hundred times. We said we could wait fifteen minutes and no more.'

'It's all gone wrong, I know it!'

'Oh, stop moaning!'

Another five minutes went by, then suddenly Lecky came running towards them from the signal up the track.

'Scatter!' he whispered. 'Something's up, and my guess is they've caught Gritz.' He reminded the others about the fifteen-minute deadline.

Joey was only too eager to get away, his growing uneasiness turning rapidly into panic. But Josh felt frustrated to have a fortune within his grasp and then to have to abandon it. Josh at least would have waited a little longer, but with the break-up of the team this was not possible. In the end, they all three piled into their van and drove away.

They didn't get far, though. For by this time the police had been alerted and had set up a road-block half a mile away. Ten minutes later, the whole gang was safely in custody.

By the time the train pulled in to Manchester Deansgate station, which was the nearest stop for the museums, the whole story had been told to an astounded Miss Pritchard and her goggle-eyed class.

'Do you mean to tell me,' she asked the railway police inspector who had now boarded the train, 'that Lenny Hargreaves, one of my less promising pupils, has actually foiled some sort of criminal?'

She was assured that Lenny had certainly had a hand in it, assisted by Jake who had had the sense to pull the communication cord. But the inspector assured her that the real heroine was Patsy Huggins, who had managed to stop an armed drug-peddling villain in his tracks without even touching

his gun.

'That was very sensible of the girl,' the inspector told Miss Pritchard. 'Guns are far too dangerous for inexperienced people to handle, and no doubt the credit for such sensible training belongs to her teacher.'

'And her mother, of course,' conceded Miss Pritchard graciously, with a smile in the direction of Mrs Huggins. The two women accepted this compliment with a pride which gradually spread its pleasure over the rest of the day. Far from punishing Lenny, Jake and Patsy for their earlier disobedience, the two women determined to turn a fairly blind eye to the children's museum antics and to let them wander off – ('Within reason, of course!') – almost as they liked. Miss Pritchard even gave Jake the money to ride on the space-flight simulator when he found he couldn't afford it after all. Lenny, however, was not pleased at the outcome of that morning's adventure. He was the hero, and he deserved all the credit. Where would any of them have been without his magic tricks? Besides, he had lost his Flying Flounder trick which Gritz had torn to ribbons, and it would take him ages to save up for another. Such a sacrifice surely deserved some special recognition? He had rescued the Spinning Spider, though, and was planning to give Patsy Huggins a neat little scare with that on the journey home, and serve her right.

By the time the Cobb Street school party moved into the snack bar for lunch Lenny had built up a great wall of resentment which kept everyone at a distance.

'He's miffed because somebody else has got a bit of the glory for once,' said Patsy's friend, Karen Cook. 'Well, it'll do him good to realise that he's not the only toffee in the jar.'

At first, those eager for more of the story had seated themselves at Lenny's table, but his sulks gradually drove them away. Even Jake grew fed up in the end and went over to talk to Erica Carr who thought he was wonderful.

Lenny had deliberately chosen a table as far away from the rest of the class as possible, and as the snack bar filled up he found himself sitting marooned among other members of the public. He began glowering round at them resentfully. Little did they know what an important person was sitting

so near to them! Well, he'd show them one day. Just wait till he had his own prime-time television programme, like Paul Daniels.

Suddenly Lenny noticed something which took his mind off his own hurt pride.

A man had come into the snack bar, carrying a cup of tea and a sandwich. This man sat down at the same table as two smart ladies who were busily chatting together. One of the ladies had set her handbag down on the table, but the other, whose bag was bigger and more like a shopping bag, had set hers on the floor by her feet. The man soon finished his sandwich, looked carefully around the snack bar, then bent to the floor and put his hand on the shopping bag. This, thought Lenny, was a highly suspicious move. Either the man meant to steal a purse or something else from the bag, or he was going to pick up the whole bag and disappear with it.

Quick as a curse, Lenny whipped out his Spinning Spider and flung it at the bag. It was a poorly-aimed throw. The spider missed the bag but landed, with its high-pitched screech, on the villain's foot. The man leapt to his feet with a cry, knocking over his chair and the remains of his cup of tea. In seconds he had left the room empty-handed.

Lenny Hargreaves was a hero once more – but an unsung hero, for nobody had realised what had happened. They had heard a strange noise, that was all. Some of them looked up, but they soon resumed their conversations. To make matters even worse,

Lenny's precious spider, kicked into the air by the frantic stranger, had fallen into the lady's open bag.

Lenny intended to go over to the ladies' table and ask for his spider back, but before he could manage it the two ladies got up and moved away. As they did so, the one with the shopping bag picked up the bill, put her hand into her bag to find her purse, and screamed the most awful scream that Lenny had ever heard.

10

Return Crisis

Lenny didn't get his Spinning Spider back, because the minute the lady screamed Miss Pritchard leapt to her feet and snatched Lenny away to her own table, assuming he had been the cause of whatever mischief had just happened. Maybe she had been too lenient with that boy today. She decided to keep a closer eye on him for the rest of the trip, and in the circumstances Lenny thought that for the moment at least it might be just as well.

But of course such close supervision soon became very boring. There were no more opportunities for mischief and the day stretched out very long indeed. Even on the way home poor old Lenny had to sit next to Miss Pritchard, while Jake sat at the table opposite them with Erica Carr. Patsy Huggins, meanwhile, was the centre of attention at the other end of the compartment. She was having the time of her life, recounting the adventure with many embellishments.

As for Lenny, it was the most boring and frustrating journey of his life. He couldn't get a word in edgeways. Jake lent him his comic, but even that didn't help because Lenny had read it already. Erica produced a Travel Scrabble set, and invited Lenny to join her and Jake in a game, but Lenny knew he couldn't spell so he loftily declined. His only hope of release was to go to the toilet, for which Miss Pritchard could not very well refuse permission.

The train had just pulled in to Welshaw station when Lenny made his request, so Miss Pritchard made him wait until the train moved off again. Then away he went, thinking he might wander off to the buffet car again. He had sixty pence left, and thought he might just be able to buy a chocolate biscuit for that.

Yet when he moved into the next compartment, all thoughts of food left Lenny's mind. For there, sitting together at one of the tables, were the two businessmen that Lenny had seen that morning, Grey Suit and Brown Suit, the latter being Mr Donald Dacre of Dacre Plastics Limited. These two men had just boarded the train at Welshaw and had settled at a table to themselves, earnestly discussing something. Intrigued, Lenny hovered discreetly nearby, intending to listen in. He was by no means convinced that these two men were as innocent as people had made out. Brown Suit in particular looked like a genuine villain to him. Fancy wearing a brown suit, for a start!

'Your poor wife! That *must* have been a shock!' Grey Suit was saying.

'You're telling me! She was absolutely distraught. I've never known her in such a state before. The very fact that she rang me up at my office was enough to show how upset she was. She knows I don't like personal calls when I'm working.'

'And you say it was some sort of trick spider that frightened her?'

'A great big enormous thing that actually made a sort of screeching noise. It might have been only a trick, but I can tell you it nearly gave her a heart attack. Linda's absolutely terrified of spiders.'

'Has she still got the evidence?'

'Oh, yes she has, don't you worry! The nasty thing was right there in her bag, and I've told her to hang on to it until we've sorted the whole thing out. For believe me, we're going to track that culprit down. He was only a kid, a schoolboy sitting by himself at the next table, but he's got to learn that he can't go around being so irresponsible and frightening people half to death. As soon as Linda screamed a teacher came and grabbed this lad. So that teacher must have known it was him. She didn't say anything, though. You'd think she could have apologised at least. And Linda was too upset to go over and speak to her. But we've got the name of the school which some of the other children happened to mention. It's a primary school over in Cobston.'

'Not the one that's on this train right now?'

'ON THIS TRAIN?' Mr Dacre's eyes nearly popped out of his head.

'Yes; and come to think of it, the same lot were travelling up with us this morning,' Grey Suit went on. 'Cobb Street Primary School. I remember seeing the name on the reservation card in the window of their coach. Didn't you say it was one of their kids

WEAVERHAM HIGH SCHOOL LIBRARY

who started the rumour that you were a terrorist? Sounds to me as if both those escapades could be the handiwork of one and the same boy.'

'That's a very interesting suggestion!' A look of strange, wild determination came over Mr Donald Dacre's face. He rose from his seat. 'If you'll just excuse me for a minute . . .' he began.

Lenny didn't wait to hear any more. He shut himself up in the toilet and stayed there until Mrs Huggins came hammering on the door to fetch him out.